story by Patricia Quinlan
pictures by John Bindon

Willy, The Champion Ant

Published in 1992 by Black Moss Press
at 2450 Byng Road, Windsor, Ontario, Canada N8W 3E8
Black Moss books are distributed in Canada and the U.S.
by Firefly Books 250 Sparks Ave., Willowdale, Ontario, Canada, M2H 2S4.
All orders should be directed there.

Black Moss books are published in Canada with the assistance of
the Canada Council and the Ontario Arts Council.

Canadian Cataloguing in Publication Data

Quinlan, Patricia

 Willy the champion ant

ISBN 0-88753-240-3

I. Title

PS8583.U345W45 1992   jC811'.54   C92-090002-X
PX0.3.Q84W45   1992

For my brother John,
with love

Sometimes I hate being an older brother; like when my sister Tasha loses my stuff.

My mom says I have to try hard to understand because she's so little.

Once, Tasha lost the baseball that I caught at a Blue Jays' game. Another time, she lost my favourite tiger's eye marble. The worst time was when she lost my pet ant, Willy.

I found Willy when I was playing marbles in the empty lot next to Mr. Emslie's service station.

My marble had rolled onto an ant hill. Willy was dragging a large piece of potato chip up the hill. I laughed when he started trying to push my marble out of his way.

I had a jar in my pocket that I was planning to catch worms in. I put the jar over the ant heap and watched Willy crawling up the sides of the glass. I decided that I wanted to keep him.

Willy and I did everything together. When my friend John and I played checkers, Willy watched.

When my mom and Tasha went shopping, I read comics to Willy at the back of the store. Spiderman was our favourite.

My mom said ants weren't allowed in bed with me, so at night, Willy slept on the window ledge in my room. "You can look at the stars if you're not sleepy, Willy," I said.

When I found Willy, I was the only kid I knew who had a pet ant. When my friends saw how much fun Willy was, they all got pet ants too. We decided to have an ant race.

The race was held on the lot beside Mr. Emslie's service station. We asked him to be the judge. We agreed to time each ant separately.

About fifty people showed up to watch the race. The Katulski kids did a great popcorn and lemonade business. The newspaper sent a reporter and a photographer.

The next morning, when I went to wake Willy up, I saw that the lid was off Willy's jar and Willy was gone. Tasha must have been playing with him and forgot to put the lid back on before she went to bed. "It's your fault Willy's gone," I shouted at Tasha.

When my mom heard what happened, she said, "We'll organize a search party for Willy." She called all the other moms in the neighbourhood. Soon, everyone was looking for Willy. Kids kept bringing ants to check to see if one was Willy.

We had to stop looking when it got dark. "We'll try again in the morning, Paul," my mom said.

Later, when I was on my way to the bathroom, I heard Tasha crying in her room. "It's my fault Willy's lost," she sobbed. "Maybe he's dead."

I hugged her. "I'm sorry I yelled at you," I said.

That night, I looked at Willy's jar for a long time. My insides felt empty like the jar.

The next day, everyone came out to look for Willy again. I heard Tasha shouting from the sandbox in the playground. "I found him. I found Willy!"

I went over to check. "Yes, it's Willy, Tasha," I said.

That night, after Tasha was asleep, my mom
came into my room.
"That was a very loving thing you did today,
Paul," she said.

"What do you mean, Mom?"

"The ant Tasha found is a brown ant. Willy is
a black ant."

My mom gave me a big hug.
"Don't tell her," I whispered.

The next day, my mom bought me a present.
It was a trophy that said, "Paul, The Champion Kid."

I keep it on my window ledge beside my new
ant. Tasha is always really careful to put the
lid back on when she plays with him. She
hasn't lost any of my stuff for at least a
month.

I miss Willy a lot. I hope he's happy
wherever he is.

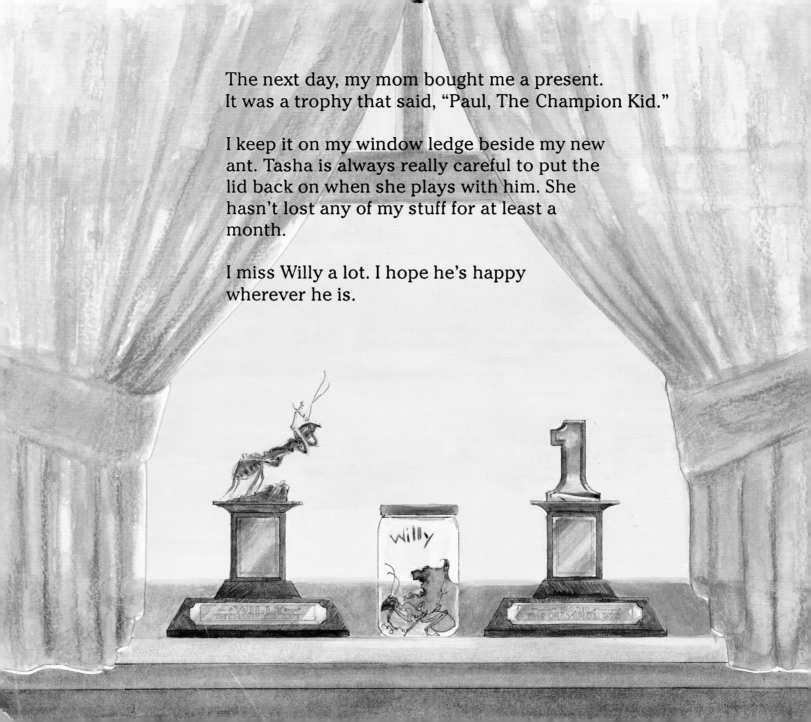